My Sister's Keeper

My Sister's Keeper

Brenda Chapman

Anna Sweet Mysteries
GRASS ROOTS PRESS

First published in 2013 by Grass Roots Press

Grass Roots Press gratefully acknowledges the financial support for its publishing programs provided by the following agencies: the Government of Canada through the Canada Book Fund and the Government of Alberta through the Alberta Foundation for the Arts.

Library and Archives Canada Cataloguing in Publication

Chapman, Brenda, 1955–, author
    My sister's keeper / Brenda Chapman.

(Anna Sweet mysteries)
ISBN 978-1-77153-004-0 (pbk.)

    I. Title. II. Series: Chapman, Brenda, 1955– . Anna Sweet mysteries.

PS8605.H36M9 2013   C813'.6   C2013-902836-6

Printed and bound in Canada.

Dedicated with love to the memory of my dad,
John Chapman

CHAPTER ONE

It was the middle of a steamy August night in Kermit, Texas, and my bedside phone was ringing. I'd worked the late shift in the Dude Bar below my hotel room, and was only just falling asleep. I felt around for the phone with my right hand, knocking an empty beer bottle onto the floor. I picked up the receiver.

"Hello?"

"You are one hard person to get a hold of," my father yelled into my ear.

"Dad? Is that you?"

I propped myself up on an elbow. I'd been in Kermit a month and hadn't gotten around to letting him know. I tried to shake off the sick feeling that came from working too many late nights.

"Of course it's me. Your sister's had an accident. She's in the hospital." He spoke matter-of-factly, but I could hear worry underneath.

"Cheri?"

"That's what I said. Your sister. Lucky she wasn't killed."

"Is she okay?"

"Yes, aside from a goose egg on her forehead and bad nerves."

I was sitting on the side of the bed now. I'd forgotten to close the curtains and the red neon sign from the parking lot flashed into my eyes.

"What...happened?"

"Brakes failed on her car yesterday on her way home from work. Cheri drove into a tree and got banged up good. She's been asking for you."

Cheri had to be in really bad shape if she wanted to speak to *me*. "I could give her a ring tomorrow," I said.

"She's waiting for your call now. Get a pen and paper."

He'd made the command with his drill sergeant voice. A voice trained by thirty-five years in the armed forces. He rattled off Cheri's phone number at the hospital. I copied it onto a napkin like an army private in his command.

Dad hung up before I could ask how he was doing. As usual, he hadn't asked me either.

· · · · · · · · · ·

Cheri picked up on the first ring, in her hospital room somewhere in Ottawa. She whispered into the phone. I could barely hear her.

"Speak up, Cheri. It's not like the FBI is listening in."

"I need to see you," she said. Her voice was just slightly louder.

My eyes travelled around my hotel room: stained red carpet, patched holes in the walls, particle board furniture. The smell of cooking grease and stale booze seeped up from the bar below. One month in this oil town felt like forever. I still wasn't sure how I'd ended up here.

"I have lots going on right now," I said. "It'll be hard to pull myself away."

Cheri didn't say anything for about twenty seconds. This time when she spoke, I didn't have to strain to hear her.

"Anna, you're the only one I can trust. You have to come home as soon as you can." Her voice dropped. "Somebody is trying to kill me. Please, Anna, you have to get on the next plane to Ottawa. If not, I'll be dead by Christmas."

CHAPTER TWO

D ad was waiting for me in the luggage claim area when I got off the plane. It was noon—just nine hours after my phone call to Cheri. I spotted him leaning against a wall, his eyes searching the crowd. His thick hair had gone completely white, but his sharp blue eyes hadn't lost their brightness. I crossed to where he was standing and stopped in front of him—the man who'd driven me crazy my entire life.

"How did you know what time I'd arrive?" I asked.

"I got here early and watched a few flights come in. You had to be on one before long."

"Well, thanks for coming."

"I could say the same."

I picked up my bags and we started for the parking garage. Dad pointed to a shiny red Ford truck. "My new baby," he said. His eyes sparkled. Some men loved women. My dad loved trucks.

He glanced over at me as we walked. "So what's so great in Kermit, Texas?" he asked.

"It's just a place. I liked the name."

He frowned. "You're what, thirty-two now, Anna? You're getting too old for this drifting around, slacking-off nonsense."

Welcome home.

"I'll have you know I'm gifted at serving beer. Plus I get to spend quality time in towns like Kermit, Texas."

"You know what I think about that."

"It would be hard not to," I replied.

We got into the truck and Dad drove out of the lot onto the parkway. The sun was beating down on the windshield. No clouds could be seen in the clear blue sky. We were halfway to the city when Dad said, "Your sister isn't herself these days."

And that's a bad thing? "What's going on?"

"She's always been high strung. Lately, she's gotten nutty. She thinks somebody's out to get her."

"What about her accident?"

He shrugged. "Accidents happen. Brakes fail all the time."

"Jimmy must be worried."

Dad shot me a sideways look. "He appears to be."

"Aren't we going to their house in Manotick?"

"Your sister refuses to leave the hospital with anyone but you. I'm going home. You can take the truck to get her."

"This truck?" I looked at him to see if he was joking. Dad never used to let anyone drive his truck—and this one was brand new.

"I got another one just like it at home."

I sat quietly for a minute. Dad turned onto his street in the south end and I saw our family home halfway down. I'd been away for five years.

"It's good to see you, Dad." I said.

Dad nodded once and turned his face away. But not before I saw a smile twitch at the corners of his mouth.

CHAPTER THREE

Cheri was dressed in jeans and a white T-shirt, her long blonde hair loose around her pale face. An angry purple and black bruise spread from a lump on her forehead. She was sitting in a chair at the foot of her hospital bed, staring at nothing, when I walked into the room. It took her a few seconds to notice me.

"Anna," she said. She opened her arms.

I walked over to her and reached down to give her a hug. I was shocked by the changes in her appearance, even though it had been five years since I'd last seen her. Her skin was dry and her eyes were listless. Even her hair had lost its shine.

I pulled over another chair and sat close to her.

"What's going on, Cheri?" I asked.

"Sometimes, I think I'm losing my mind." Her blue eyes filled with tears. "I can't sleep. Crazy things have been happening to me. I'm so scared."

"Where is Jimmy? Shouldn't he be here with you?"

The tears began to slide in twin rivers down her cheeks. "Jimmy moved out two months ago. We were fighting all the time. He had to take Evan because I'm such a mess."

Their five-year-old son, Evan—I'd seen him once as a newborn. The news of Cheri and Jimmy's marriage troubles might have given me pleasure once, but not now.

"Dad could have driven you home."

"Dad doesn't believe me. He thinks I'm making it all up, and I can't . . ." Her voice trailed away.

"Are you still working?" I asked.

She shook her head. "I'm on stress leave. I was going to be made partner in the law firm, but now... I'll be lucky if they keep me on."

So whatever was wrong with her had been going on for a while. Cheri had always liked drama but never to this degree. I slapped my knees with both hands and stood up.

"Let's get you home and settled before someone shows up with a needle and a bedpan." I used the same cheery voice to clear drunks out of the bar at closing time.

I helped Cheri to her feet. She leaned against me and we started for the door.

I thought about how she was lucky to only have suffered a bump and a headache when her car hit that tree. "We'll get through this," I said to her. Even though I hadn't wanted to come home, I added, "Whatever you need, I'm here until we sort it out."

Cheri pulled me back and made me face her. "I'm sorry," she said, wiping away more tears.

"For what?"

"For picking Jimmy over you. You won't believe how many times I've wanted to say that to you. You deserved better from both of us."

I stood stock still. I'd die for my sister, but she'd strained our bond to breaking many times. Jimmy had been the biggest betrayal along a string of others since our childhood.

"It's okay," I said, happy to realize I meant it. "I've moved on. Let's agree to just put the whole thing behind us."

"I've missed you."

I knew she meant the words when she said them. I also knew our truce wouldn't last long. It never did, but I hoped our new-found closeness would be enough to carry us through whatever nastiness was to come.

CHAPTER FOUR

We smelled something rotting as soon as we stepped inside the house. I turned to Cheri, who was following me like a shadow.

"Your power must have been off. You could have a fridge full of ruined food."

"Whatever is causing that smell is disgusting. Phew."

I looked around Cheri and Jimmy's house. It was an older bungalow on a two-acre lot in Manotick, a village a half-hour outside the city. Oak floors and cream-coloured walls made for a warm front hall. Cheri had always liked the finer things in life. I spotted expensive-looking paintings and leather furniture on our way to the kitchen.

Cheri crossed to the fridge and opened the door. She turned to look at me. Her face made it clear she was puzzled. "That's odd. The food in the fridge is fine." She checked the garbage under the sink. "Nothing here either."

A shiver travelled up my spine, even though it was warm in the kitchen. Maybe it wasn't rotting food that we were smelling. "I could use some tea," I said. I sent her a shaky smile. "Why don't you make a pot while I go to the washroom?"

"If you like."

I made my way down the hall, checking each room as I went. The guest bedroom looked fine and the bathroom was clean. That brought me to the master bedroom. The smell was getting stronger. The door was half shut. I slowly pushed it open. My breath caught in my throat.

The bloody carcass of a small animal lay squarely in the middle of Cheri's bed. White maggots crawled all over its rotting flesh. The duvet cover was stained dark red. I forced down my breakfast, then slammed the door and leaned against it. I tried to still my pounding heart.

Cheri appeared at the end of the hallway, holding two different packages of tea. "Would you like mint or..."

She stopped talking and looked at me. Her pale face got even whiter.

I took a step toward her. "I think we should call the police," I said calmly. "Somebody has left a dead animal on your bed. By what's left of its fur, I'd say a raccoon. Likely roadkill."

Cheri's eyes got wide and her mouth opened in a silent scream. I almost reached her before she slid into a heap on the floor. I crouched down next to Cheri and checked her pulse. It was beating like a jackhammer.

She came to quickly. When she looked up at me, her eyes were panicked. She grabbed my shirt and pulled my face close to hers.

"We can't call the police," she begged. "Jimmy will know. All the cops look after each other. You know that."

"It might not be Jimmy doing this." Not the Jimmy I remembered.

"He's the only one with a key to the house."

"Then, we'll prove it's him."

"Not if his cop friends get involved. Promise me you won't call them."

I tried to calm Cheri down but she got even more upset. Finally, I agreed to keep the dead raccoon a secret, against my better judgement.

"I'm going to get the locks changed while you have a nap in the spare room," I said. "I'll get rid of the dead animal right after I find a locksmith. It means a drive to the nearest mall to find a dumpster. But the smell is only going to ripen, and you'll thank me later." I wondered how long I could hold my breath. "I sure hope you own a full can of air freshener," I said. "And a full bottle of Scotch would come in handy too, for when I get back."

CHAPTER FIVE

I bagged the raccoon and bedding and opened all the windows. After dumping the bag in the garage, I sat at Cheri's kitchen table thinking about Jimmy Wilson. We'd met at the Orillia police academy almost twelve years ago. I was attracted to his wide smile, curly black hair, and Irish charm. Jimmy was the kind of guy who lit up a room and worked it like a movie star. I felt like the luckiest girl alive when he zoomed in on me.

Four years after we started dating, Jimmy asked me to marry him. We'd both gotten jobs on the Ottawa force and we'd put a down payment on a house in Sandy Hill. I was twenty-four and head over heels for him. That loving feeling died, however, when he slept with my twenty-two-year-old sister, Cheri. I was working a night shift. Cheri was visiting for the weekend.

For three years after their wedding, I avoided my fiancé turned brother-in-law while we worked in the same unit on the Ottawa force. I always made sure Cheri and Jimmy weren't at my father's before I went to visit. I stopped dating altogether.

Footsteps in the hallway pulled me back into the present. Cheri had climbed out of bed and was crossing to the bathroom. A few minutes later, she joined me at the kitchen table. She looked terrible, and had spidery red lines criss-crossing the side of her face she'd pressed into the pillow.

I pushed a notepad and pen in front of her. "I'll make coffee, and you write down everyone in your life: names, relationship to you, possible motive. We have to treat this like a real investigation."

"Even if Jimmy is the only suspect?"

"Even if."

She lifted the pen and began writing. Her other hand cupped her chin, her elbow resting on the table. I made the coffee strong and sweet. I set cups on the table and sat next to her.

"Have you defended any unhappy clients?" I asked.

"I defended a nineteen-year-old for dealing drugs. He's serving eight years. His father was angry and said I should pay for not getting him off."

"What's the father's name?"

"Gavin Long. He used to belong to a biker gang."

"Lovely. Write him down." I looked at the list. "There are six people in your law office?"

"Yes. The owner Bob Cahill, me, and two newer lawyers, Hannah Jones and Roger Little. We have one legal assistant named Janet Chan and an office manager, Betty Zimmer."

"And you were being made partner?"

"Yes. I earned it too." Her jaw jutted out. It was a defiant look I knew only too well. "I worked long hours and took on tough cases. Our firm is doing very well. We plan to move to a bigger office in a few weeks. We're holding interviews for two more junior lawyers."

"What about affairs? Are you or Jimmy involved in one?"

Cheri lifted her big blue eyes to mine. We both knew what I was thinking. Both of them were capable. "I'm not," she said. "But Jimmy could be. I think that's one of the reasons he moved out."

"You're not sure?"

"No."

I made some notes next to the names she'd written down. I was quite certain her doctor, dentist, hairdresser, and manicurist were not out to kill her, but I would check them out too. "Is there anything else you need to tell me?" I asked.

Cheri nodded. "I started getting phone calls in the middle of the night right after Jimmy left. At first they hung up without saying anything. Then, they'd tell me my life was going to end soon. I also started getting emails at work that said awful things, like Evan and Jimmy were better off without me. I began thinking I was being followed. Sometimes, things were moved around in my office or at home. I thought I was losing my mind."

"When they phoned, was it a man or woman?"

"I couldn't tell. I'd be half asleep and they spoke so low."

"What about the emails—did you get a return address?"

"They were from a Gmail account with no name. I printed the emails and filed them away at work. Then I deleted them. They made me sick. One said that if I told anyone, Evan would disappear."

"I'm going to start at your office. I want to read those emails."

Cheri stood up. "Then I'm coming with you."

CHAPTER SIX

Cahill Law Office was located on the tenth floor of a downtown high rise. Jada Price, a former classmate of mine at the police academy, was the security person seated behind the desk at the front door. She took one look at me and said, "Well I'll be. It's Anna Sweet in the flesh. You look good, girl."

"And so do you," I said.

Jada had let her hair grow into an Afro and she looked fierce—liquid black eyes and a short, muscular build. Jada once told me that her great-grandparents were slaves in the Southern States and she'd inherited their physical strength. She'd even trained as an Olympic hurdler. But she missed out on the games because of an injury.

Jada's eyes darted between me and Cheri. She knew our history. "How you doing, Cheri?" she asked. She didn't give Cheri a chance to respond. "Up to any police work, Anna?" she asked.

"No," I said. "I've been working in bars across the U.S. I plan on hitting Asia next."

Jada shook her head. "Such a waste of your talents." She looked around the lobby. "And mine."

"I thought you got a job with the Ottawa force," I said.

"I got sick of being the token black girl handing out parking tickets. I quit two years ago. I've only worked security the last year, while getting some things in order."

Cheri had drifted over to the elevators. "Well, good seeing you, Jada," I said. I signed the visitors' book and followed Cheri.

"Jada didn't make any friends while she worked for the police," said Cheri as the elevator door closed. "Jimmy told me that she spoke her mind too much. She even accused one of the officers of sexual harassment. They were happy when she quit."

"Which officer did she accuse?"

"Jimmy never said."

I took out my notepad. "Looks like we just found another name for your list."

· · · · · · · · · ·

The office manager, Betty Zimmer, was a tiny woman about sixty-five years old. She greeted Cheri warmly and said she was relieved to see Cheri back at work. "Would you like some tea?" she asked. "My, that's some lump on your forehead, Cheri dear."

Betty didn't seem to realize that we were sisters. Most people didn't know we were related when they first met us. I was five foot nine with a mess of dark hair and dark brown eyes. Cheri was petite, curvy, and blonde with china blues. Betty must have assumed I was her client.

Cheri kept walking with her chin up in the air. "No tea, Betty." She ignored the comment about her injury.

We passed by an office and two surprised faces turned toward us. I correctly guessed they were Hannah Jones and Roger Little—the two other lawyers on staff. Both were dressed in expensive navy suits and stylish glasses. Hannah stood first and came to give Cheri a hug.

"So good to see you back," Hannah said. "Are you recovered from the accident?"

Roger gave Cheri a quick hug. "We've been very worried about you." He was tall and lean with a shaved head. I pictured him on a bike pedalling for a finish line after a six-hour triathlon.

Hannah and Roger stood looking at me through their designer glasses. Roger's eyes were intense, like those of someone who had a religion they wanted you to join. I held out my hand.

"I'm Anna Sweet," I said. "Just visiting Cheri." I shot Cheri a look to keep her mouth shut about us being sisters. Luckily, she had taken Jimmy Wilson's last name when they married, so my last name was different from hers.

Cheri played along. She pointed toward her office. "We came by to pick up a folder but I'll be off the rest of the week. I plan to be back in the office soon, though."

"Why, that's wonderful," Hannah said. "We've missed you around here." Hannah wore her red hair in a tight bun and appeared to be an expert with the makeup brush. Her eyelids were dusted in blue shadow and her lips were glossy pink. She was attractive if you liked that straight-laced, librarian-in-a-tight-skirt look.

"I hope you haven't had to take on too many of my cases," Cheri said. "I felt bad leaving you both with extra work."

"We enjoyed the challenge," Roger said. "I went to court the last few weeks and got two of your clients off fraud charges. Both of them were probably guilty. But it was fun convincing the judge they weren't."

"You should have seen Roger in action," Hannah laughed. "He danced circles around the prosecution."

"It was great fun," said Roger. "So you're really feeling better, then, Cheri? We'd heard that you were having a rough go." He rubbed his hand back and forth across his bald head while he spoke. His eyes stared at the lump on Cheri's forehead.

"I'm much better now, thanks," Cheri said. "Is Bob in?"

"He's having a meeting with Janet," said Hannah. "They're working on the office move."

Bob Cahill, boss, and Janet Chan, legal assistant—I remembered their names from the list. They must have heard our voices because they both suddenly appeared from his office. They took turns hugging Cheri. Cheri introduced me as her visiting friend.

Bob was another tall man, but older than Roger and with a full head of white hair. "So when will you be back?" he asked Cheri after shaking my hand.

"I'm hoping by the start of next week," she said. She was putting on an Oscar-winning performance.

Nobody would believe this was the same pale, frantic woman I'd sat with a few hours earlier.

A look passed between Bob and Janet. The look was personal: the kind shared by two people who are jumping each other's bones. I would bet money that they were more than just boss and legal assistant. She was short with black hair to her waist. Attractive if you like that temptress-in-a-low-cut-top look.

Bob cleared his throat. "We are looking forward to your return, Cheri. I've put a few new cases on hold for your review."

"I can't wait to come back," Cheri said, smiling. "I'll be rested and raring to go."

CHAPTER SEVEN

Cheri collapsed against her seat and closed her eyes. She looked drained of energy. I reached over and patted her knee.

"Well played, sister," I said. "Dad would be proud."

She turned her head to face me and grinned. "Never show your underbelly. If you're hurting, suck it up. Act like a champion and you'll be one."

I started the truck. "If we had a dollar for every time he drilled that into us."

"We could retire in style," said Cheri. "Where to next?"

"Your place. I need some sleep and so do you. Tomorrow is going to be a big day. I'm going to track down the other people on your list."

"I could come with you," Cheri offered. She shivered.

"I thought you could stay with Dad for the day. I'll move around better alone. You'll be safe with him."

"Won't that be fun." Cheri sounded like she'd just been told to eat her broccoli, but there was relief too.

I looked at her and grinned as I backed out of the parking spot. "Won't it, just?"

I drove slowly, checking in the rear-view mirror to see if anyone was following us. At one point a white van was keeping two car lengths behind our truck. I started to get worried but it made a right turn at the next set of lights. I sped up the last stretch of highway into Manotick. Cheri's house was at the other end of town near the river. Homes there were expensive and far apart, with large lawns and lots of trees and shrubs—older homes that took more than a week to put up.

We were pulling into Cheri's driveway when she said, "I miss Evan but if I try to get him away from Jimmy, I don't know what Jimmy will do. At least his energy is focused on hurting me and not Evan. He's always been a good dad."

"It might not be Jimmy trying to hurt you."

"I know you hope so. I really want you to find that someone else is behind this. But in my heart, I believe it's Jimmy. He has lots of reasons to want me gone from his life for good."

"Now why would you say that?" Cheri had faults, but Jimmy had known about them before he married her.

"We were fighting...a lot. He was tired of me working all the time. I can't tell you how many times he said I was neglecting Evan. We fought over money, too. He said I was putting us into debt, as if my jewellery and clothes were the problem."

Cheri never had been good at finding fault with herself. I could understand Jimmy's frustration. Yet, he had married her, warts and all.

"You said that you thought he was fooling around on you. Who do you think he's been seeing?"

"Somebody at work, but I don't know who. It took me a long time to believe he would do such a thing."

Did you forget that he was engaged to me when he had a go at you? I managed to keep the thought from leaving my mouth.

"If Jimmy *is* behind all of this, I'm going to find out and make him pay. You can count on it," I promised. "Can you open the garage door? I want to hide Dad's truck so Jimmy doesn't find out I'm here yet."

• • • • • • • • • •

Cheri and I ate a cheese and mushroom pizza that she had in her freezer. Then we got ready for bed. I decided to sleep on the couch in the living room. I wanted to be able to move around during the night to keep watch. The couch was angled, so I could see the front door and the hallway leading to Cheri's bedroom. She was still in the guest bedroom. She'd sleep there until she got a new mattress for the master bedroom. The raccoon's blood had permanently stained the old one.

I waited until Cheri was safely in bed with the light off before I pulled out the folder of emails from her office. The first was a warning. It was dated June 10, two months ago.

If you say anything to anybody, Evan will disappear.

The emails got more and more disturbing. The last two must have destroyed Cheri.

Have you thought about killing yourself?
Maybe you should.
Evan will be better off when you are gone.

I counted a total of sixteen emails over eight weeks—sixteen nasty pieces of mail to make my sister go crazy. Combined with the late-night phone calls, they'd been a powerful weapon. When the first email arrived, Jimmy had already moved out and Cheri was depressed and hurting. Soon after the emails and phone calls started, she couldn't even cope with looking after Evan. That's when she took her stress leave from work.

The person behind this harassment was a sadist in my books. They were also a coward. Jimmy had been a lot of things when I knew him. He was never cruel or a coward. Could somebody really change that much in five years? Had the mean streak always been part of him?

I reached over to turn out the table lamp and snuggled under the blanket. I could never remember being this tired before. My mind had been working overtime since I got Dad's phone call. I'd been running on adrenaline.

I started to drift off. Right about now, the bar band would be starting up in the Dude Bar. The night's action would be just getting under way. I wondered if my bar regulars missed me in Kermit, Texas. I sure didn't miss them.

I listened for unusual noises outside the house. All was quiet except the wind rattling the windows. I let myself relax. I'd get a good night's sleep and recharge. I was going to need my body firing on all its engines if I was going to have a chance of unmasking the real Jimmy Wilson.

The retired cop in me was looking forward to the challenge.

CHAPTER EIGHT

Saturday morning started off warm and sunny. Clouds and rain would be rolling in late afternoon, according to the weather channel. I drove Cheri to Dad's around ten.

"I phoned Dad before we left the house. He's invited us for supper," Cheri said as she opened the car door. "He plans to make ribs with his special sauce."

"I'll try to make it," I said. "If I don't, save me some."

Cheri stepped out and leaned into the car. Her hands rested on the roof and door. She was wearing a Mickey Mouse T-shirt and a baseball cap. With her hair tied back in a ponytail, she looked way younger than thirty.

"It feels good to have someone believe me. You have no idea."

"I think I do."

"Be careful, Annie."

"You too."

I'd planned to follow Jimmy to work when I woke up. Then I remembered that he worked different shifts. Cheri had phoned the station to find out his schedule for me. Sure enough, he was on night shift and would be sleeping now. His mother Bonnie took care of Evan when Cheri and Jimmy both worked. Cheri said that it was easy for Jimmy now since they'd moved into Bonnie's house. I'd swing by later in the afternoon.

Gavin Long was first up on my list this morning: former biker gang member and father of drug-dealing son Joey, now doing serious time. I'd looked Gavin's address up on the internet before leaving Cheri's. I'd also found news articles from the trial. It would be about a half-hour drive to the east end of the city. What better way to start the day than by spending time with this fine, upstanding citizen who'd threatened revenge on my sister?

··········

The man who opened the door to the two-storey Cape Cod home was not what I expected. For starters, the tattoos, chains, and leather that gang members favoured were nowhere to be seen. Instead, he was wearing a white cotton shirt and khaki pants, and his grey hair was cut short. He was also leaning on crutches, his foot in a cast. He looked me up and down with calculating black eyes.

"I'm sorry to bother you," I said, smiling. "I'm writing an article about parents who have kids in jail, possibly for crimes they did not commit. Your son's name came up in my search."

"How did you find my address?"

"Canada 411."

He stared at me, weighing my words to sniff out if I was lying. Finally, he laughed and opened the door wider. "Why don't you come in and we can talk, sweetheart? I'm having a hard time standing since I broke my foot two weeks ago."

He led me into a back sun room and we each sat down in a rattan chair. The room was hot, a ceiling fan bringing little relief. He moved his left knee so that it was almost touching mine.

"How did you hurt your foot?" I asked.

"Running from a pretty woman. I wouldn't run from you though," he said.

"That's because your foot's in a cast." I took out a notebook and pen.

He laughed. "You're one tall, cool drink of water. What is it you want to know for your article?"

"How did you feel when your son Joey was found guilty of drug trafficking?"

He scowled and I saw the thug lurking below the surface. "How do you think I felt? I was angry. The lawyer should have gotten him off, because my boy was innocent. Make sure you print that."

I wrote his statement down and nodded as if he'd said something important. "Who was the lawyer defending him?"

"Some dumb blonde. I forget her name now. It was some kind of bimbo name."

Cheri, maybe? "Wow, she sounds bad. What's happened to her career since?"

Gavin's hand landed on my knee. "Why do you even care about her? The real story is that my son is doing time and he's innocent. Justice was not done."

It wasn't wise to keep pushing, but I made one last attempt. "I just think I could make her pay for doing such a bad job defending your son."

"Don't worry your pretty head. She's already dead to me. I've hired a new lawyer to get my son out on appeal."

Dead to you? What did that mean? I didn't dare ask anything more about Cheri. He'd get suspicious, and I'd be watching my back for the rest of my life.

"Did you want to say anything else about the trial or the legal system?"

He showed me his teeth in what passed for a smile. "Nothing you could print."

"Well, thank you so much for your comments. I'll be sure to send a copy of my article to you if they print it."

His eyes narrowed. "What's the name of the paper? You never said."

"I freelance. I write articles and submit them to every paper going. One of them usually takes it, but not always."

I watched his hand start moving up my leg toward my thigh. I resisted the urge to kick him. Instead, I stood in one quick motion and smoothed down my shirt.

"I'm sorry to take up so much of your time," I said. "I have someone waiting for me in my car. They're probably baking in the heat by now. Thank you again. I'll see myself out."

"You know where I live," he called as I hurried for the door. "Come see me anytime you're out this way. We could do some partying."

"Sounds good," I yelled back to him. "Thanks again."

I walked as fast as I could to the truck, which I'd parked out of sight around the corner. Gavin Long might be harassing Cheri, but he honestly seemed to have forgotten her name. Even though I couldn't cross him off the list of suspects, he wasn't as high up as he had been. However, if being a creep got you arrested, he'd be sitting in a cell doing life with no chance of parole.

CHAPTER NINE

I stopped off at Whispers Pub in Westboro, in Ottawa's trendy west end. I found an empty table on the patio in the shade of an umbrella. The lunch hour was over and people at a few tables were paying their bills. The waitress came over after they left. I ordered tomato soup and a grilled cheese sandwich and a beer. Then I sat back and people-watched.

I could hardly believe my eyes when ten minutes later I looked over and saw Ryan Hunter standing at the entrance to the patio. I knew he lived up the street but never thought I would run into him. The last time I'd seen Ryan, he was lying in a hospital bed with a bullet in his leg and another in his chest. He walked with a cane now. It had been five years since we'd been partners. He'd aged a lifetime since then. It made me want to punch something. Fear of facing him kept me in my seat with my head down.

The waitress returned with my beer and food. I sipped from my glass just as Ryan slid into the seat across from me. He leaned his cane against the wall and grinned.

"The one and only Annie Sweet. When did you get back into town?"

"Yesterday. It's good to see you, Ryan. Been a long time." I waved at the waitress. "Another beer for my friend."

"You quit the force," he said. He sat back and looked at me.

"Yeah." Quitting wasn't something I liked to talk about.

"You never were one for talking about yourself," he said, as if reading my thoughts. The waitress set a beer in front of him. Ryan raised it in my direction. "To old partners."

I clinked his glass with mine. "To old partners." We both took a long drink.

"How've you been?" I asked.

"Good, believe it or not. I had to quit the force —you know, after the shooting—but there *is* life outside it. I got a part-time job at a local youth centre. I'm also working on an English degree." His eyes were steady on mine.

"No way."

"It was something I always wanted to do. I'm majoring in British poetry."

"You amaze me, Hunter. You really do."

"What have you been up to, Sweet?"

"Nothing so grand. I've worked all around the U.S. Seems every town is crying for another waitress." I shrugged. "Not much else worth speaking about."

"I wanted to see you after I got out of the hospital. Your dad told me you'd left town. Said you were on the move. He's a crusty one, by the way."

"He is that." I took a bite of my sandwich.

"Anna, what happened?"

I looked at him, or tried to. I swallowed before speaking. "You know what happened. You pulled the kid's attention away from me over to you. You took two bullets because I didn't act fast enough."

"But you shot him and saved my life."

"I was nearly too late. He almost killed you while I hesitated. The stupid thing was that I didn't shoot at first because he was a kid. I let my feelings get in the way. He would have shot me—and you—dead without batting an eye."

"The boy was out of control before we got there. You tried to talk him down. He might just as easily have put down the gun."

"But he didn't. The internal review finished me. I couldn't face you afterward. I had to get away and do something mindless."

"They found that you weren't at fault."

"I know what they found." *And I'm done talking about it.*

I went back to eating. We chatted about how much the city had changed, people we knew and places I'd lived. Ryan finished his beer. He set the empty glass on the table.

"Well, I'm meeting a friend inside the pub." He stood and looked down at me. "I hope to see you again before you leave the city."

"I'd like that."

I stood and he reached for me. We hugged each other hard. "Don't keep running, Sweet," he whispered into my ear. "Forgive yourself. You're a good cop and should get back in the game."

CHAPTER TEN

At two o'clock, I parked the truck across from Bonnie Wilson's house on Royal Avenue. I picked a spot behind a blue Mazda a few houses down. I still had a good view of her front door and was out of sight. I tried to make myself comfortable. It would be a couple of hours before Jimmy left for his five o'clock shift.

He didn't know I was back in town. So I could secretly tail him for a bit and hope he tried something. Catching him in the act would give me the upper hand. I admitted that it was a long shot.

Sitting in the truck, I thought about Ryan Hunter. We'd been partners for nearly three years. I'd just finished training and he'd already put in twenty years on the Ottawa force. We were a good team—until we got the call to stop a drugged-up kid from shooting his gun from the roof of his garage. The kid had nearly killed my partner before I'd shot him dead. I'd lived with killing that fourteen-year-old boy every day since. And I'd lived with letting my partner down.

It was nearly four thirty when a black Volvo pulled into a spot in front of the Mazda. I slumped down in my seat without taking my eyes off the house. A woman in a tight skirt and high heels stepped out of the car. She crossed the street toward the Wilson house. Something about her looked familiar. She climbed the front steps and rang the doorbell. After about a minute, the door opened.

Jimmy stood there with a cup of coffee in one hand. He was in his police uniform. His hair was still black and curly. He smiled and I saw a flash of the charm that had won me over so many years ago. He said something, and then a five-year-old boy appeared next to him. *Evan, my nephew.* I'd only seen him as a baby. I leaned forward. Evan was tall for his age and blond like Cheri. Even from this distance, I could tell that he had her big eyes. He was a good-looking child.

The woman bent and talked to Evan. Jimmy checked his watch and must have told her that he had to leave for work. The woman stood up and patted Evan on the head. She and Jimmy talked for a few seconds before she turned and walked down the steps. Jimmy disappeared inside, and his mother Bonnie took his place next to Evan and shut the door.

Too many people around to have a private talk, Jimmy? I wondered. *It's hard to carry on an affair with your mother and son standing next to you.*

I looked again as the woman crossed the street to her car. My eyes widened in surprise. The red hair and designer glasses could only belong to Hannah Jones, the lawyer in Cheri's office. She'd just walked up to Jimmy's door as if she knew the way, as if they knew each other. Why was Hannah visiting Cheri's husband before his shift? Was something going on between them? Jimmy hadn't cared for my feelings when he dropped me for my sister. He wouldn't care if he dropped Cheri for her co-worker.

"Once might be a mistake," I said out loud. "But twice is a pattern."

CHAPTER ELEVEN

Jimmy left for work five minutes later. He drove directly to the station, with me a few car lengths behind him. It was Saturday so traffic was light.

I found a parking space on Elgin Street in front of the station. I sat in Dad's truck and thought about what to do. I could walk in and confront Jimmy, or I could check out Hannah Jones. Tracking down Hannah seemed like the better idea. I'd find out more about her before I faced Jimmy.

I'd have to do a search on Hannah to find out where she lived. I could follow her to see if she met up with Jimmy after his shift. Maybe they were making plans to meet when I watched them on Jimmy's front steps.

I had a few hours to kill. I'd go to Dad's for supper and use his computer to do a search. I didn't even own a cell phone, since I rarely called anyone. It would have come in handy now. I'd also try to find out more about Hannah from Cheri. The trick would be not letting Cheri know why I was interested.

I drove slowly east toward Bank Street. I'd follow it south to Dad's. My mouth watered at the thought of his ribs. I used to dream about them when I was on the road. Sometimes, I woke up thinking I could taste the smoky BBQ sauce.

Other nights, I woke up dreaming about a fourteen-year-old kid dying on the pavement in front of me. Those dreams were the ones that kept me going from town to town. They were the ones that kept me from coming home.

···········

I pulled into Dad's driveway and noticed his other truck was gone. It was silver with a cab and bigger than the one I was driving. I entered his house by the back door. I was sure Cheri would be working on supper but it was Dad who stood stirring something on the stove. The kitchen smelled of ribs and sauce. A bowl of steaming mashed potatoes sat on the counter.

"Good. One of you made it on time," Dad said.

"Where's Cheri?" I asked.

"She went for a drive a couple of hours ago. She told me she'd be right back."

"She didn't say where she was going?"

"Not to me."

"Maybe I should go look for her."

"Where would you even begin? Come and eat before the meal gets cold. She'll be here when she gets here."

"I'll call her first," I said. Worry made my voice hard. Cheri had said she wasn't going to be gone long. Anything could have happened to her.

Dad handed me two plates from the cupboard. "I already called and her phone is turned off. Let's eat."

We sat at the table and served ourselves. Dad opened a couple of beers and handed me one. We drank out of the bottles. I tried to calm the worry in my belly and started eating. It was hard not to enjoy the spicy ribs and creamy potatoes.

"So, you home for a while?" Dad asked.

"I'm not sure. Once this business with Cheri is settled, I'll probably head right out again."

"Well, might be good if you stuck around a while." He threw a stripped rib bone onto his plate and picked up a fresh one. "Cheri hasn't been the same since you left."

"I can't be responsible for her happiness."

"I know. I'm glad you've come to help her now. Even if she doesn't deserve your forgiveness."

"I'm over Jimmy, Dad."

Dad chewed another rib and drank from his beer bottle. "She had to give up Evan. Court order. She's not allowed to see him alone."

I lowered my fork. "You're kidding me."

"I wish I was. She left him in a park and forgot all about him. Jimmy had a search party out looking for him. It took Cheri a long time to come down off whatever drug she'd taken to tell us which park."

"Cheri doesn't take drugs." *Does she?*

"She swore up and down she hadn't, but she was upset. Jimmy had just moved out. Excuse me." Dad stood to answer the phone.

I wasn't hungry anymore. Something very ugly was going on with my sister. Could she have caused her own car accident? Maybe she'd even put the roadkill on her bed. She might be trying to look like a victim to get Jimmy and Evan back. She might even be mentally ill. I guessed it was an option I was going to have to consider.

I heard Dad say goodbye and hang up the phone. I looked over. He stood in the doorway to the kitchen, his face white. "That was Jimmy. A woman's body was just found outside Cheri's house. He's on his way there now. Maybe we should make a run over."

I'm sure my face went as white as his. "Let's not jump to any conclusions," I said. "Cheri might just be late for dinner." I tried to sound calm.

Neither of us believed me for a minute.

CHAPTER TWELVE

I drove. Dad and I didn't talk. We were each getting ready to face what lay ahead. The sun had started to set. Every so often, rays of light blinded me through the windshield. Shadows stretched across the road.

Cheri's street was filled with cop cars and an ambulance. Red lights were flashing and people were standing in a group watching police unroll yellow tape. A body lay on Cheri's lawn under a white sheet.

I spotted Jimmy with his back to me. He was talking to another cop. I needed to get his attention but would have to get past some of the police officers.

"Anna," Dad said. "I'll stay here. You go and find out."

"Okay, Dad. I'll be right back."

He nodded. Dad stood straight as a rod, as if at attention in a military lineup. His eyes stared directly ahead to the body on the ground.

I slipped under the tape and ran toward Jimmy. Someone grabbed my arm but Jimmy had turned. His eyes opened wide and he signalled for the cop to let me go. Jimmy walked over to me.

"Anna. I never expected to see you."

"Is it … is it Cheri?" I asked.

"No." His eyes looked past me to where Dad stood. Jimmy shook his head so Dad would know it wasn't Cheri.

"Who is it?"

Jimmy looked at the sheet on the ground then back at me. "It's someone Cheri works with."

"Who?" My mind scrambled over the people I'd met.

"Her name is Hannah Jones. Somebody struck her with a car and she flew several metres onto the lawn. The car must have been going full out."

"Did you know her?"

"I met her at a few of Cheri's work parties. I wouldn't say I knew her." He avoided my eyes and looked past me. "Mr. Sweet. I'm sorry to have gotten you out tonight."

I turned and saw that Dad was right behind me. He looked relieved but upset. He shook his head. "I'm sorry for the family of the young lady under that sheet. But I'm glad it's not my girl."

I took his arm. "I'll take you home, Dad. Cheri should be there by now." I turned to Jimmy. "You and I have to talk. I'll be by in the morning."

I wanted to find out why Jimmy had lied. Hannah had visited him at home that morning. They knew each other better than he had let on.

....

Cheri was sitting at the table reading the newspaper when Dad and I walked into the kitchen. She took one look at our faces and her smile disappeared.

"Where have you been?" Dad asked. His voice was gruff.

"Just out." Cheri said. "I picked up the car from the mechanic and drove around for a while. He's doing an oil change on your truck, Dad. My treat. We can pick it up any time. Anyhow, I lost track of time. Has something happened?"

"Talk to your sister," Dad said to me. "I'm going to pour myself a Scotch and watch some television." He grabbed a glass from the cupboard and went down the hall to his den. My father avoided family upsets whenever possible.

I sat down across from Cheri. "Really, where have you been all this time? You have to tell me now if you did anything wrong. I'll try to help you."

"You're scaring me."

"This isn't like when we were kids. You won't be able to bat your big blue eyes and get away with whatever you did."

"How did you know?"

"Oh crap." I'd been hoping I was wrong. I sighed. "Did you mean to hit her?"

"What are you talking about? I know that I didn't tell you everything and I'm sorry, okay?"

"Walk me through it."

"I'm not allowed to be with Evan unless someone else is there. I did something crazy after work one day. I picked him up and don't remember anything after that. I have no idea why I left him alone in a park. I blanked out."

"Dad already told me that. Did you blank out again today?"

She raised her head and looked at me. "No. I knew where I was."

"Tell me exactly what you did."

"I picked up my car from the garage. They'd fixed the brakes and the damage to the hood and bumper, you know, because of the accident. Then I drove over to Evan's school. I waited outside until he came out. I watched him play during recess. I knew I should just leave but I followed his bus home. I got out and called to him. He ran into my arms and I hugged him. Bonnie came out and yelled at me. Then I let him go and drove back here." Cheri started crying. "I miss him so much."

"Are you telling me you didn't drive to your house in Manotick?"

"Why would I go there?" Cheri wiped her cheeks with the back of her hands. She looked confused.

I stared at her for a bit. She either: (a) didn't have anything to do with Hannah's hit and run accident, (b) had lost her mind, or (c) was a great actress.

"What's Hannah Jones like?" I asked.

"Hannah? She's smart and ambitious. She's the new breed of young lawyer—wants to get to the top right away. They don't put much stock in experience. She and Roger Little are a lot alike in that way."

"Did Jimmy know Hannah very well?"

"No. They met at a few of my work parties, but that was it. Why?"

"Hannah was killed outside your house in Manotick today, Cheri. She was hit by a car. The driver fled the scene."

"No!" Cheri looked around the kitchen. Her eyes were round blue pools of fear. "Jimmy must have mistaken her for me." Her voice dropped to a whisper. "I should have been the one to die. Oh my God. Hannah Jones died instead of me!"

CHAPTER THIRTEEN

I banged on Bonnie Wilson's door at eight the next morning. After a minute, I leaned on the doorbell. My nephew Evan opened the door still dressed in his pyjamas. He carried a plastic water pistol.

"I'm here to see your dad," I said. "My name is Aunt Anna."

Evan studied me with Cheri's blue eyes. "Dad's sleeping. Are you my aunt?"

"I am. Can you go wake your dad up for me? Maybe give him a big blast of water from that gun you're carrying."

"Okay."

Evan scooted down the hall and up the stairs. I smiled when I heard Jimmy shriek. Bonnie's angry voice travelled downstairs.

Ten minutes later, Jimmy joined me where I was sitting on the front steps. He wore a black T-shirt and jeans. His eyes were red and tired. His black curls could have used a good brushing. "I worked late," he said. "I need coffee."

"We could walk to the Baker Street Café."

"Sure."

He trudged along beside me. Neither of us said much. Mornings had always been our worst time. I needed coffee as badly as he did.

The café was busy, as it usually was Sunday mornings. We got a table near the back and both ordered bacon and eggs. We were on our second cup of coffee when I started asking questions.

"So what's going on between you and Cheri?"

Jimmy sighed and leaned back in his chair. "Cheri and I started fighting last year. She was working all the time. When she wasn't working, it was all she talked about. I thought if I moved out, she'd rethink things. As it turned out, she started acting out, wanting my attention. Do you know she even took drugs and left Evan alone in the park? I wanted to strangle her."

"You might want to watch how you phrase things."

"She refuses to talk to me."

"Could it be because you took Evan away?"

"She was acting crazy. I had to make sure he was safe."

"What about Cheri? Do you care if she's safe too?"

Jimmy rolled his eyes. "You mean the supposed phone calls and threats? She's just trying to get my attention, as I said before."

"She thinks you're trying to kill her."

"Like I said, she's trying to get my attention. You know what she's like."

An unspoken thought passed between us. Yes, I knew what my sister was like. All our lives, Cheri had wanted what I had and she had found ways to take it. She had to be the centre of attention. Jimmy was living proof.

"I don't think that's what's going on," I said. "She honestly fears for her life. She thinks you want to get rid of her."

"Do you believe that, Anna? You know me as well as anybody. Do you honestly think I'm capable of killing my wife?"

"You tell me. What was going on between you and Hannah Jones?"

"Hannah Jones? Nothing. What makes you ask me about her?"

"Because I saw her at your house yesterday morning. Maybe that's why you'd like to get rid of Cheri. Maybe Hannah was going to tell Cheri about your affair, so you got rid of her first. Hannah could make your divorce very messy. Plus, it wouldn't be the first time you dropped a woman when you'd had enough of her."

"Ouch." Jimmy winced. "Nobody was more surprised than me to see Hannah yesterday. She wanted to meet after I finished work to tell me something. Then she ended up dead on our front lawn. With all the crazy things Cheri's been up to ... She might have thought we were having an affair too, and done something about it. I can't even go there. I have nothing more to say."

The waitress set our plates of food in front of us. We stared at each other for a good long time and then dropped our heads to eat. I knew from what I'd just read in Jimmy's eyes that he was done talking.

Later when I drove the truck back to Dad's, I remembered the Jimmy I'd planned to marry. I could tell that he felt something for me still. The eyes never lie. Not for the first time, I wished I'd stayed far, far away from Ottawa. When this was over, I'd be making tracks to Kermit, Texas, as fast as the plane could fly me. I owed myself that.

No ties. No problems. Nobody to cause me grief ever again.

CHAPTER FOURTEEN

Monday morning, Cheri pulled herself together. She got up, put on her navy suit and high heels, and got ready for work. She put blush on her cheeks to cover up her pale skin. Some magic cream covered up the dark circles under her eyes. Her jaw jutted out in its old defiant way.

"If I stay at home much longer, Bob Cahill's going to give someone else my promotion. I need to spend time with my co-workers. It's still so hard to believe Hannah is dead."

"What about your fear that someone tried to kill you?" I asked.

She smiled. "Jimmy called me last night. He said that I can see Evan if I'm feeling better and not acting so ... crazy."

"That's big of him, but he might still be trying to hurt you."

"I don't know. Jimmy didn't sound as angry with me as he has been. He even said he missed me. Evan keeps asking to come home."

"And that's it? You don't fear for your life anymore?"

A shadow of worry passed across Cheri's eyes. She shook her head as if clearing away bad thoughts. "Maybe I went a little overboard. I'm putting all that behind me."

"And what if you weren't imagining the danger?" Jimmy might be trying a new approach if he'd had a hand in Hannah's death.

"The emails started when Jimmy and Evan moved out. Whoever is behind this, if there is anybody, will stop when my family comes home."

I stared at her, too stunned to reply. There were only two reasons that I could see behind her change of heart. Either Cheri was choosing to believe what she wanted to believe, or she was the one behind all the nastiness. Both options were disturbing.

A memory of eight-year-old Cheri flashed across my mind. Our mother had been dead three weeks and Cheri hadn't cried. In fact, she hadn't asked what happened to our mother. I was only eleven years old but even I found my little sister's reaction odd. One day after school, I walked past Cheri's bedroom. She was talking on the phone to her best friend Emily. Cheri was telling Emily that our mother would be home from the hospital as soon as she felt better.

Dad took Cheri to the doctor after that. The doctor said that Cheri knew deep down that Mom was gone forever. But she coped by making up a story that allowed her to feel safe. She would accept our mother's death when she was ready.

Cheri's biggest fear had always been that people would desert her. She feared that the people she loved would leave her even more than she feared that her husband could try to kill her.

··········

For the next two weeks, Cheri left for work each morning by nine and returned for supper at seven. I fell into the role of shopper and chef. I listened carefully over plates of pasta, chicken casseroles, and grilled steak as she told me the details of her day. I listened for lies and watched for signs of craziness. I thought about booking that plane back to Kermit.

And yet, something didn't sit right. I knew my sister. Her panic had been real. Sometimes, I could still hear the fear just beneath the surface of her words. I couldn't leave her alone just yet. The case didn't feel closed.

I spent my days researching everyone in Cheri's life, including her co-workers and neighbours. I found out some interesting information, but nothing that screamed killer.

Cheri's boss Bob Cahill was married with four daughters—two in university and two in high school. His wife's parents owned real estate. Someday, she was going to inherit a fortune.

Bob hired Janet Chan as his legal assistant a year ago. Twice a week, they spent their lunch hour at the Blue Rock Motel. I tailed them four times and waited outside. Whatever they were up to lasted forty-five minutes. Bob always left ten minutes before Janet.

Roger Little, the other young lawyer, grew up in Montreal and studied law at McGill. He wasn't married and spent his free time playing squash and training for Iron Man competitions. He and Hannah Jones had dated off and on. They met in law school. They didn't appear to be a couple when she died.

Betty Zimmer, the sixty-five-year-old office manager, lived with her son in the south end. She was divorced and just scraping by. She spent her free time at bingo and church.

None of Cheri's co-workers had a criminal record. And they all seemed crushed by Hannah's death.

··········

Dad dropped by to see me two Thursdays later. I made coffee and we sat on lawn chairs in Cheri's backyard. August was nearing an end. I'd been in Ottawa almost four weeks now and was getting restless. Mornings were chilly and the afternoon heat had ended. Still, it was comfortable drinking our coffee in the sun on the deck.

"How's Cheri?" Dad asked. "Has she got her head screwed on straight again?"

"Hard to say. She's working long hours and comes home too tired to do anything. I've become her cook and cleaner."

"She has a way of turning events in her favour. Sometimes I think I was too easy on her after your mother died."

"Yeah. Well, since I've been here, she hasn't gotten any late night phone calls. No threats of any sort. Jimmy thinks she made it all up. What do you think, Dad?"

"Hard to know. Seems a bit over the top, even for Cheri." He studied the string of pine trees at the back of the yard. "Although she was mighty worked up when Jimmy left."

"Cheri and Jimmy have been talking a lot lately. They talked last night about having dinner as a family on Sunday. Cheri says Jimmy wants to try again." I looked at my father. "I'll be leaving soon. I've got an open-ended plane ticket back to Kermit."

Dad nodded. "Thought as much." He turned and looked at me sideways from under the brim of his ball cap. "You know you could stay with me if you want."

"Thanks, but when I move out of Cheri's, I'll be on my way south." I paused. "What would you think about Cheri telling people I've left town? I could lay low for a few days at her place. If somebody is waiting for a chance to torment her, they might think the coast is clear."

"If there is anyone."

"And if not, we've nothing to lose."

Dad turned his head away from me and thought it over. "I guess there's no harm in it if Cheri agrees. We could put this all to rest before you head off again. Either the nut will come out of the woodwork, or Cheri has given up acting like someone's out to get her. With a chance of Jimmy and Evan returning, she's getting what she wanted. My money's that she returns to normal."

"You're probably right. Although Cheri and normal aren't two words I'd use together as a rule."

Dad smiled. Then his face turned serious. "You're sure Cheri's front bumper was free of damage?"

"Not even a scratch. It was replaced after her accident with the tree. Any damage would have been easy to spot. She didn't hit Hannah Jones with her car. There'd be evidence."

Dad sighed. "I'll be really happy when all this is over."

"You and me both, Dad."

CHAPTER FIFTEEN

Jimmy was in his office at the police station when I dropped by. He looked good in his dark blue uniform. Too good. He was working at his computer. He looked up when I knocked. His face broke into a smile.

"I can't stay," I said. "I'm just heading out of town."

"You stayed longer than I thought you would. Where are you going now?"

"Back to Texas. I like the heat in the winter. Plus I have a good job waiting for me."

"Cheri told me you're working in a bar." He grinned.

"Not just any bar. This one serves dudes." I waved my hand toward the door. "My plane leaves in a few hours but I wanted to say goodbye." Lying to Jimmy felt good.

Jimmy stood. He made like he was going to hug me. I turned and rushed out of his office as if I hadn't noticed.

· · · · · · · · · ·

My next stop was Cheri's office. A plump man with white hair was working the security desk. I stopped in front of him.

"Is Jada Price on a day off?" I asked.

"Jada's quit. She handed in her notice last week. You want me to tell her anything from you?"

"Just tell her Anna Sweet said best of luck and goodbye. I'm heading back to Texas."

The guard looked at me over the top of his glasses. "Anna Sweet you said? Jada asked me to give you her card if you came by. She wants you to call her."

I took the card and tucked it into my pocket. "Thanks. I'm not sure I'll have time this trip. Maybe next time I come back."

· · · · · · · · · ·

Betty Zimmer was packing up a box of files when I walked into the main office. "We're moving to a bigger office next week," she said. "Three new lawyers are starting and we're so busy. You can go right in. Cheri's in her office."

"I've just dropped by to leave Cheri her house key. I'm heading home to Texas in a few hours."

"Texas? How lovely. I have a sister who lives in Miami. I plan to move there when I retire next year."

"You won't miss the snow."

"I should say not."

Cheri came out of her office. "So, you're on your way?" she called as she walked toward me.

"Yes, my plane leaves in two hours. I just wanted to return your house key. Thanks for putting me up the last few weeks." I spoke loudly. The offices were close together and I had no doubt everyone could hear me. I could see Roger Little and Janet Chan working at their desks. Bob Cahill's office door was partly open.

Cheri hugged me. "I'm going to miss you."

"You'll be too busy to miss me."

Cheri laughed, loud and happy. "You're probably right."

She linked arms and walked me to the elevator. "How'd I do?" she whispered.

"Perfect. See you at home."

"I'll be leaving here around six."

"The pork chops will be soaking in sauce and ready to grill."

CHAPTER SIXTEEN

I hid out in Cheri's house the entire day and night. It felt like a police stakeout, something I hated more than handing out parking tickets. The time went slowly without incident. No late night phone call. No threatening emails. I began to think Jimmy might have been right. Cheri had made up a crisis to get attention.

When Cheri came home the next evening at seven, I was going stir crazy.

"Will you be okay if I go for a jog before dinner?" I asked.

"Go ahead. I'm going to have a shower. Then I'll pour a glass of wine and work until you get home. What smells so good?"

"I've made a lamb stew in the slow cooker. It will be ready when we want to eat."

"I had a late lunch with Jimmy and Evan. I'm not hungry yet." She smiled. "They're moving back home on Saturday."

"That's two days from now. That's quick."

"I told Jimmy I wouldn't work as many hours. We have three new lawyers so my workload is lifting. And I promised to take a family holiday now that my promotion is final."

"Did you tell him I'm still here?"

Cheri shook her head. "I haven't told anybody."

"I'll book my flight when I get back from my run. I'll catch a flight Saturday morning."

Cheri took off her suit jacket. She dropped it on the back of a chair. "Did Dad tell you anything about his health?"

"No. Is something going on?"

"He'll be angry if I say anything." She started walking out of the kitchen. She unbuttoned her shirt as she went. I followed her down the hall into her bedroom.

"You can't just say something like that and leave me hanging. Is Dad sick?"

"The doctors are running tests. Nothing is certain yet."

My heart felt like it was being squeezed. "He never said anything about not feeling well."

"You know Dad—a soldier to the end. He really will be angry if he knows I told you anything."

"Well, thanks ... I think."

I left Cheri and went into the spare bedroom. I pulled on some shorts, a T-shirt, and a hoodie, then tied up my runners. At the last minute, I grabbed a baseball cap and tucked my hair up underneath. I pulled the hood over top. Darkness was setting in. Still, I wanted to make sure nobody could recognize me. Pretending Cheri was living alone probably didn't matter. But I'd give my plan two more nights.

"I'll lock the back door," I called to Cheri. She was just getting into the shower. "Back in about an hour."

"Take your time," she called.

I stepped onto the deck and locked the back door. Already the air was cooling down. A breeze had blown in clouds from the west. I looked into the sky and sniffed the air. Rain was coming but a ways off yet. I should have lots of time to get in my run.

I stretched on the lawn in the shadows. I slipped out the side gate and ran down Maple Street, past the park toward Prince of Wales Drive. Manotick was a growing town trying to hang on to its village charm. I followed the side streets at a slow pace, taking time to look at yards and late-summer gardens. Old oak and maple trees lined the roads. Hardly any cars passed me and I enjoyed the silence. A cool wind pushed me along, making the jog easy. My body felt lighter just being outdoors in the fresh air.

I used to run marathons and work out in the gym. After leaving Ottawa, I stopped running and working out. I stopped just about everything, including keeping in contact with my family and friends.

My father had always seemed like a rock. I wasn't sure how I felt hearing that he might be sick. The idea that he might even die was too much to swallow. I picked up my pace.

A man walking his collie came toward me. I'd never seen him before and nodded as we passed each other. Another block further on, I checked my watch. I'd been running just over half an hour. The shadows had been replaced by complete darkness. I took the next street back toward Cheri's house. I'd left her alone long enough.

CHAPTER SEVENTEEN

I didn't notice anything out of order...at first. I took a few minutes in the backyard to stretch. I could see through the patio doors into the kitchen. Cheri wasn't sitting at the table but a file was open. An empty wine glass sat next to it.

I climbed the steps and took out my key. The door was still locked. I opened the door and stepped inside. The house was quiet and still. I figured that Cheri must have gone for a nap and shut the door as quietly as I could. I slipped off my runners and padded over to the sink for a drink of water. Halfway to the sink, I stopped and looked over at the table. Something was out of place.

A second wine glass sat on the table. From the angle I'd looked in through the window, the glass had been hidden behind a vase of purple coneflowers. The glass was half filled with white wine.

Cheri hadn't said that company was coming over. I pictured the road in front of her house and the driveway. The only parked car was Cheri's. So two questions: who had dropped by and why hadn't they finished their wine?

I turned back to the sink but something else caught my attention: a folded sheet of white paper with Jimmy's name on the top. I hesitated. If Cheri hadn't shown such bad judgement lately, I wouldn't have even thought about reading it. But these were crazy times.

I moved closer and picked up the paper. I held it for a few moments, then flicked it open. My eyes skimmed the typewritten words with a signature written in pen. I stopped and read it again more slowly.

Jimmy,

I'm so sorry for what I am about to do. I've been depressed since you and Evan moved out. Life will never be the same, even if you both move home. I can't stop thinking about you with Hannah Jones. I didn't mean to do it. Please forgive me for everything. You and Evan are better off without me.

I will love you always,

Cheri

It was my sister's signature all right. However, the message was crazy. She hadn't been depressed an hour ago. In fact, she'd been excited about Jimmy and Evan moving home. She also seemed to be saying in the note that she'd killed Hannah Jones over her affair with Jimmy. At one point, Cheri had thought Jimmy might be having an affair with someone at his work. If she'd suspected Hannah, she would have told me. I hadn't told Cheri about Hannah's visit to Jimmy before the hit and run ... or after. Plus, Cheri's car had not hit Hannah. *Details.*

I looked at the second wine glass again. Cheri had let somebody into the house. They'd sat here and shared a glass of wine. It must have been somebody she knew and trusted. Where could they have gone? If her death was meant to look like a suicide, the killer would have to come back to wash out their glass.

A muffled crash from beneath my feet made me jump. They were still in the house! I walked quickly and silently down the hall toward the front entrance.

The door to the basement stood open.

CHAPTER EIGHTEEN

I'd seen enough horror movies to know the evils that could await you in the basement. I took a moment to return to the hall closet. I picked a nine iron from Cheri's golf bag and started down the stairs. The stairs were carpeted and I was able to step silently to the bottom. I kept to the wall, hoping I wouldn't be seen.

The main room with the wide screen TV and sound system was empty. I stood still for a moment and listened. Someone was talking from the direction of the furnace and laundry rooms. The doorway was to my right. I lifted the golf club up to my shoulder.

I angled my head around the corner of the laundry room and took a quick look. This room was empty. I stepped inside and crossed to the next doorway. A man's voice grew louder. *Please not Jimmy.* I still couldn't make out what he was saying.

I crept closer, keeping to the wall. The man's back was to me in the middle of the room. His bald head shone in the ceiling light. Cheri was sitting on the floor across from the doorway. Her back was to the wall. Terror filled her eyes as she watched Roger Little loop a short rope through the I-beam that ran across the nine-foot ceiling. He'd placed a chair next to him. A hunting knife lay on the seat.

"Just another minute," he said. His voice was friendly, almost kind. "This may not snap your neck, but you'll strangle soon enough."

"I still don't understand," Cheri said. She whimpered.

Roger laughed as if they were sharing a joke. "It's simple. I want to be partner. I convinced Hannah that I could drive you out of the agency. She went along with it for a while. It was working too. You should never have come back from stress leave."

"Hannah was in on this?"

"Oh yes, but she started getting cold feet when I drugged your tea and your kid got left in the park. She got *really* bummed out when I cut your brake line. She thought I'd gone way too far when you ended up in the hospital. But I was just starting to have fun."

"You nearly killed me."

"I know! Who would have thought that I'd enjoy myself so much? The rush I got from breaking you down was incredible, even better than winning a triathlon. It became like a game. Some nights I couldn't sleep, planning my next move. Anyhow, Hannah was going to tell you and your husband everything. I was sorry to kill her. But she would have ruined my career."

He finished tying the knot and tested the hold. "That should about do it. I'm just happy you've played crazy so well. You fell for every trick I thought up. Although I was disappointed that the raccoon didn't have a bigger impact. I was hoping it would send you into a mental hospital. After all, I went to a lot of trouble to copy your house key. Scraping a dead raccoon off the highway was no picnic either."

He bent and picked up the knife. "Time for you to say goodbye. I promise you, it will be quick. I'll say some nice words at your funeral. Maybe I'll even get Cahill to put up a picture of you in the waiting room when I'm made partner."

That's when I lunged forward with the golf club pulled back to swing. Roger had begun to straighten and turned toward me as I flew the short distance toward him. His eyes went from happy to shocked.

The club cracked him with full impact just above his left ear. He crumpled into a heap on the floor.

"That quick enough for you?" I asked.

CHAPTER NINETEEN

Roger Little was handcuffed and placed under arrest. Then he was carted off to the hospital on a stretcher. Officer Peter Tang guided me into Cheri's living room to get my statement. Cheri was taken into the kitchen for hers, once she assured us that she wasn't hurt. I was constantly amazed at how she could pull herself together. She had an untapped well of grit in her, just like Dad.

Jimmy burst through the front door as I was finishing up. He looked terrible.

"Anna," he said. His voice came out strangled. "Where is she?"

"Cheri's in the kitchen. She's not hurt."

"Are you okay?"

"I'm fine. Go see Cheri."

"Thanks." He rushed past us and disappeared into the kitchen.

I turned to Tang. "If you're done with me, I think I'd like to get some air."

He closed his notebook. "Sure. Will you be staying here?"

"No, but I'll let you know where I am."

I walked out the front door. It was past midnight. I hadn't expected to be greeted by reporters and a TV camera. Two women came at me with microphones. I looked past them at my father leaning against his truck. One of the officers had called and told him what had happened, and that Cheri and I were okay.

"No comment," I said. "I was just called to the scene."

"You weren't the one who saved..." The woman looked at her notes. "Cheri Wilson from being killed."

"No. You've got me mixed up with somebody else."

I walked past them to my father. "Hey, Dad."

"I was going to come in but it seemed better to stay out of the way once I heard you were both okay."

"Jimmy just arrived. He's with Cheri."

"I saw that. You want to spend the night at my place?"

"If you don't mind."

"I don't mind. I'll talk to Cheri tomorrow."

"Yeah. I don't think she's going to miss us tonight."

We got in the truck. I leaned against the head rest and closed my eyes. I was suddenly so tired I couldn't keep my eyes open.

"I made the bed up in your old room," Dad said. "You can stay as long as you like." He put the truck into gear. "Good job you have that stubborn streak. You were the only one not to give up on your sister."

"I almost did."

But this time I hadn't walked away.

• • • • • • • • • •

It was just past three o'clock two days later when I entered the bar. A few men sat at tables drinking beer. I searched in the corners. Jada Price waved and I walked over to her table near the exit.

"Thanks for coming," she said. She'd gotten rid of her Afro and her hair was short and layered. The style suited the strong bone structure in her face. Silver hoop earrings sparkled in the light. "I was happy to read in the paper you hadn't left the city. Hard to believe that Roger Little was stalking

Cheri. I never liked the look of the guy. There was something in his eyes when he looked at me."

I sat across from her. The waitress came over and I ordered a beer. Jada was drinking something pink in a tall glass.

"So how's your sister?" she asked.

"Cheri has already put her near death behind her. Jimmy and Evan are back. She has a promotion at work. Life is back going her way and God is in his heaven." I smiled out of the side of my mouth. "I hope that didn't come out bitter."

"And what about you?"

"I've decided to stick around for a bit. Keep an eye on my dad and make sure he's eating his vegetables." The waitress set a beer in front of me and I paused to drink. "He's waiting on some follow-up test results from the cancer clinic."

"Sorry to hear that. Waiting is the hardest part." Jada leaned closer. "Well, I want to make you a job offer. As you know, I stopped working security at Cheri's building. I've started up a private eye agency. I figure it's a two-person operation. Are you interested in coming on board as my partner?"

"I'm rusty at police work. Rusty nails and other Scotch-based drinks are another matter."

"You'd have to get a PI licence. I'd need you to get started on it right away. Work has been coming in."

I stalled for time. "What would we call ourselves? Ebony and Ivory?"

"Maybe something a little less diverse. Does this mean you're in?"

I took another sip of my beer while I thought it over. My father wasn't getting any younger. Even if he wasn't sick this time, he could be down the road. Kermit, Texas, would always be there. And it might be nice to get to know my nephew Evan before he went off to college.

"I'll sign on for a year," I said. "If you're good with that, we'll have another meeting when the year is up to see if it's working out."

Jada stood and let out a whoop. "I am very good with that." She pumped her fist and sat back down. She raised her glass toward me. "Here's to us, Anna girl. You and me are going to take this city by storm."

"Storm Investigations," I said. "It has a certain ring."

"Strong and hard to predict," Jada said. "I like it. Here's to Storm Investigations."

I lifted my glass and clinked hers. "To Storm Investigations." I drained the rest of my glass.

A full year in Ottawa.

Part of me liked the idea of taking on cases. Another part wanted to get on the next plane out. I raised my hand to the waitress and called for another round.

I'd made my decision. Now I'd have to live with it for a year. I just hoped the year wasn't one I would live to regret.

ABOUT THE AUTHOR

 Brenda Chapman is a popular mystery author. The *Jennifer Bannon Mystery Series* is aimed at young adults while the *Anna Sweet Mysteries* are for adults. Her novel, *The Second Wife,* was short-listed for the Golden Oak Award in 2011. A former teacher, she now works as a senior communications advisor in Ottawa.

ALSO BY BRENDA CHAPMAN

In Winter's Grip
The Second Wife
Second Chances
Could Mourning: A Stone Child and Rouleau Mystery

Jennifer Bannon Mystery Series
Running Scared
Hiding in Hawk's Creek
Where Trouble Leads
Trail of Secrets

You can visit Brenda's website at
www.brendachapman.ca